D1808034

USBORNE HOTSHOTS
DINOSAURS

USBORNE HOTSHOTS
DINOSAURS

Edited by Lisa Miles
Designed by Karen Tomlins

Illustrated by Luis Rey, Bob Hersey,
John Shackell, Val Biro and Stuart Trotter

Photographs by Howard Allman

Series editor: Judy Tatchell
Series designer: Ruth Russell

CONTENTS

What were dinosaurs?

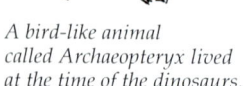

Dinosaurs were a group of reptiles which lived from around 200 million to 65 million years ago. This means that there were dinosaurs on Earth for around 135 million years, which is 70 times longer than the time people have existed. The name dinosaur means "terrible lizard".

A bird-like animal called Archaeopteryx lived at the time of the dinosaurs.

Dinosaur types

There were lots of different types of dinosaurs, but they did not all live at the same time. Some were massive plant-eaters and others were big, fast hunters. Others were tiny, no bigger than a cat.

What is a reptile?

A reptile is an animal which has scaly skin and produces its young by laying eggs. Reptiles are cold-blooded which means that they cannot control the temperature of their bodies. Their body temperature is the same as the environment around them. Animals such as lizards, snakes and crocodiles are reptiles.

The lizards of today, like this American fringe-toed lizard, are relatives of the dinosaurs.

This is a Deinonychus. It was a fast, fierce hunter.

How do we know?

Scientists called paleontologists search and dig the Earth's surface looking for the remains of bones and teeth from long-dead animals. These remains are called fossils. How fossils are made is explained on page 8.

Many remains of dinosaurs have been found buried in rocks, including their bones, skin, eggs and even footprints. From this evidence, we can tell what dinosaurs were like and also about how they lived.

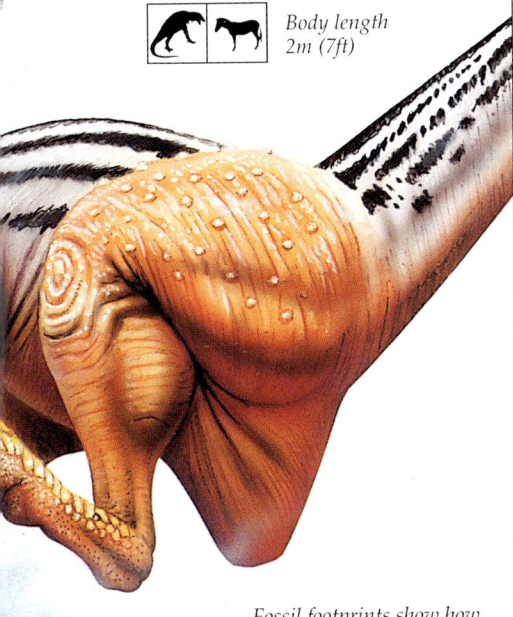

Body length
2m (7ft)

Fossil footprints show how quickly dinosaurs ran. Fast runners left footprints that were far apart.

Scale boxes

The boxes beside each illustration compare the size of a dinosaur with another animal. The animals used for comparison are shown below.

Mallard duck,
length 60cm (2ft).

Zebra, length
2 – 2.5m (7 – 8ft).

Crocodile, length
4m (13ft).

Giraffe, height
4 – 5m (13 – 16ft).

Elephant, length
6 – 7.5m (20 -- 25ft).

The really large
dinosaurs are
compared with
a truck, length
15m (50ft).

Where dinosaurs came from

Over millions and millions of years, plants and animals change and develop. This process is called evolution. Dinosaurs, like all life on Earth, evolved from very simple lifeforms. Early life developed in the sea, because the land was too hot.

Early sea life

550 million years ago, the land was hot and lifeless, but the seas and lakes were full of plants and animals.

For millions of years, the seas stayed warm and calm. Creatures with outer shells developed and then creatures with backbones. As more time passed, fish developed. The first fish were jawless, but later fish had jaws with sharp teeth.

Opabinia (oppa-bin-ya) – a sea creature from 500 million years ago.

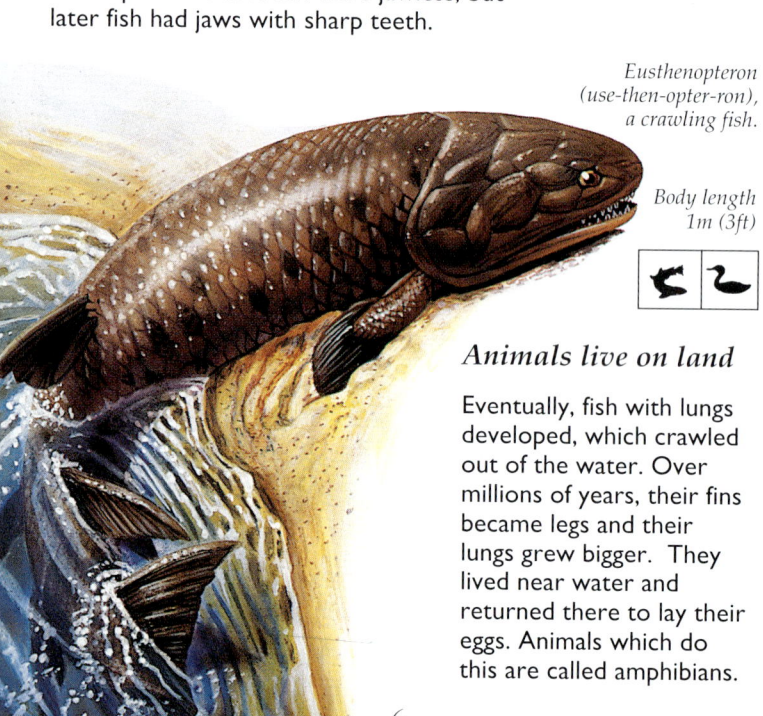

Eusthenopteron (use-then-opter-ron), a crawling fish.

Body length 1m (3ft)

Animals live on land

Eventually, fish with lungs developed, which crawled out of the water. Over millions of years, their fins became legs and their lungs grew bigger. They lived near water and returned there to lay their eggs. Animals which do this are called amphibians.

The reptiles arrive

Around 280 million years ago, it became very hot and dry in many places on Earth. The ponds and swamps dried up and most of the amphibians died out. At this time, a new kind of creature developed – the reptile.

Reptiles had waterproof, scaly skin and laid eggs on land in warm sand or in nests made of rotting plants. The eggs were protected from the hot sun by a leathery shell.

Large "fin" on back helped to keep the reptile cool by releasing heat from the body into the air.

Body length 3m (10ft)

Dimetrodon (dee-mee-tro-don) – an early reptile.

Archosaurs

One particular group of reptiles, called archosaurs, appeared around 230 million years ago. At first they were large, crocodile-like animals with bony plating covering their bodies and tails. Later they evolved into the dinosaurs.

Short arms with grasping hands.

Body length 3m (10ft)

Long legs for running after prey.

The archosaur, Ornithosuchus (or-nith-oh-sook-us).

Fossil clues

If something died on land, its body was eaten or it rotted away. If it died near water, it might be preserved as a fossil, as described below. A fossil shows the shape of an animal or plant preserved in rock. The only way to learn about extinct creatures is to find and study fossils.

Coral fossil from the Devonian period, 395-345 million years ago.

How was a dinosaur fossil made?

1. The dinosaur's body sank to the bottom of a swamp or was washed into a lake, where it also sank. Over long periods of time, the body was buried underneath layers of sand and mud, called sediment.

2. The dinosaur's soft flesh gradually rotted away, leaving only the hard skeleton. Over thousands of years, more layers of mud built up and the weight of these layers turned the mud into rock.

3. The buried bones of the dinosaur were gradually filled or replaced by minerals, which hardened into a fossil which was shaped exactly like the original bone.

4. The Earth's surface has always moved slowly – bending, folding and buckling. As it moved, the layers of rock containing fossils also moved. Some of them were pushed up to the surface to form dry land.

5. Wind, rain and sea gradually wear away the Earth's surface and fossils in the rock are sometimes exposed and discovered. If an exposed fossil lies undiscovered, it too will wear away and be destroyed.

The imprint of a bivalve shell in limestone.

Sea urchin from the Jurassic period, 195-135 million years ago.

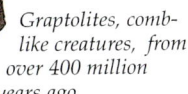

Graptolites, comb-like creatures, from over 400 million years ago.

Crab

An ammonite, a shelled animal now extinct. The picture shows a cast of a fossil rather than the fossil itself.

Paleontologists have found fossils of many different plants and animals, many now extinct.

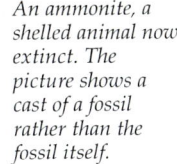

Coral

Discovering dinosaurs

Some museums display dinosaur skeletons which have been put together using fossils. The skeleton on display is probably made using plaster casts of the actual fossils.

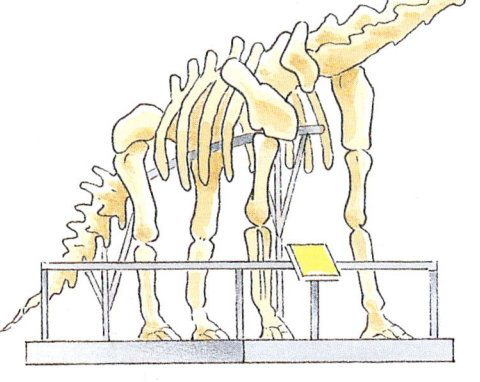

This dinosaur skeleton in a musuem shows a Diplodocus (see pages 14-15).

If some bones are missing from the fossilized skeleton, experts have to imagine what they looked like.

The first dinosaurs

The first dinosaurs lived in the Triassic Period of life on Earth, which began around 225 million years ago and lasted until 195 million years ago. At this time, the Earth's climate was warm and dry.

Lesothosaurus

Body length
90cm (3ft)

Lesothosaurus
(less-oh-toe-saw-rus)

This dinosaur was small and slender. It had small grasping hands and a horny beak which it used to nip off leaves and shoots.

Coelophysis
(see-low-fie-sis)

This was one of the first meat-eating dinosaurs. It lived around 215 million years ago. It had a slender, lightly built body and bird-like feet. It probably ate insects, lizards and perhaps smaller dinosaurs.

Powerful back legs.

Sharp claws to hold prey.

Body length
2m (6½ ft)

Heterodontosaurus
(hetter-roe-donta-saw-rus)

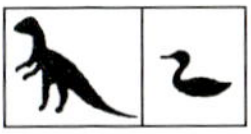

Heterodontosaurus was a light and fast-running plant-eater. It had powerful arms with sharp claws, and tusks in both jaws. It used these to defend itself.

Body length
90cm (3ft)

*Males had tusks
in their jaws, for
fighting.*

Plateosaurus
(platty-oh-saw-rus)

This dinosaur lived in herds and normally walked on all fours. It was a plant-eater and could stand on its back legs to reach leaves on trees. It was one of the first large dinosaurs.

*Rows of
sharp teeth
cut plants
into little
pieces.*

Body length
6m (20ft)

*Its tail helped
Plateosaurus
to balance.*

How big were they?

This diagram shows how big some of the first dinosaurs were compared with a person.

Plateosaurus

Coelophysis

Heterodontosaurus

11

Dinosaur food

Animals that eat meat are called carnivores, while animals that eat plants are called herbivores. Like other animals, dinosaurs were specially adapted for the kind of food that they ate.

The meat-eaters

Carnivorous dinosaurs had long, sharp claws for attacking their prey and pointed teeth for tearing meat. Many of them were large and bulky.

Others chased their prey at high speeds, running and leaping using their long back legs. Deinonychus (die-nonny-kus) was one of the fastest and fiercest meat-eaters.

Deinonychus had powerful, snapping jaws.

Strong claws held onto struggling prey.

Body length 2m (7ft)

The meat-eater *Compsognathus* (comp-sog-nay-thus) was one of the smallest dinosaurs ever. It was no bigger than a cat and it ate tiny animals.

Compsognathus chasing a lizard.

Body length 60cm (2ft)

The plant-eaters

The herbivores did not all compete for the same food. Giant dinosaurs ate leaves in the treetops, while small dinosaurs ate plants on the ground. The giant dinosaurs must have eaten enormous quantities of leaves every day, just to stay alive.

Many plant-eaters, like this Apatosaurus, had long necks for reaching tall trees.

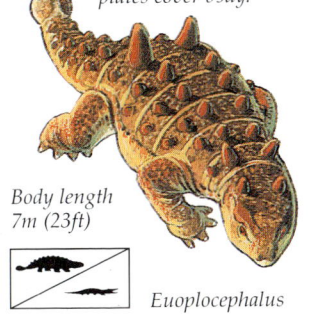

Spikes and bony plates cover body.

Body length 7m (23ft)

Euoplocephalus

Fighting off the carnivores

Some herbivores lived together in packs to defend themselves from carnivores. Others, like this *Euoplocephalus* (you-oh-plo-seffa-lus), had spikes or heavy plating on their bodies to ward off enemies.

The herbivore *Paleoscincus* (see page 22) had another way of defending itself. It could ward off attackers by whacking them with the bony club on the end of its tail.

Giant dinosaurs

The biggest of the dinosaurs were the largest land animals that have ever lived. They were all plant-eaters and spent much of their time in swamps, where the water supported their huge bodies, and they were safe from meat-eaters. They belong to a group called sauropods.

Brachiosaurus
(bracky-oh-saw-rus)

This dinosaur weighed almost as much as two elephants. Unlike other sauropods, its front legs were taller than its back legs to help it to support its great weight. It had an extremely long neck for reaching the tallest trees.

Long front legs

Shorter back legs

Body length 23m (75ft)

Diplodocus
(dip-low-doe-kus)

Diplodocus measured 28m (92ft) from its nose to the tip of its tail. It used its massive tail as a whip to defend itself. The brain of *Diplodocus* was no bigger than a hen's egg, though.

Body length 28m (92ft)

Diplodocus had a sharp claw for fighting.

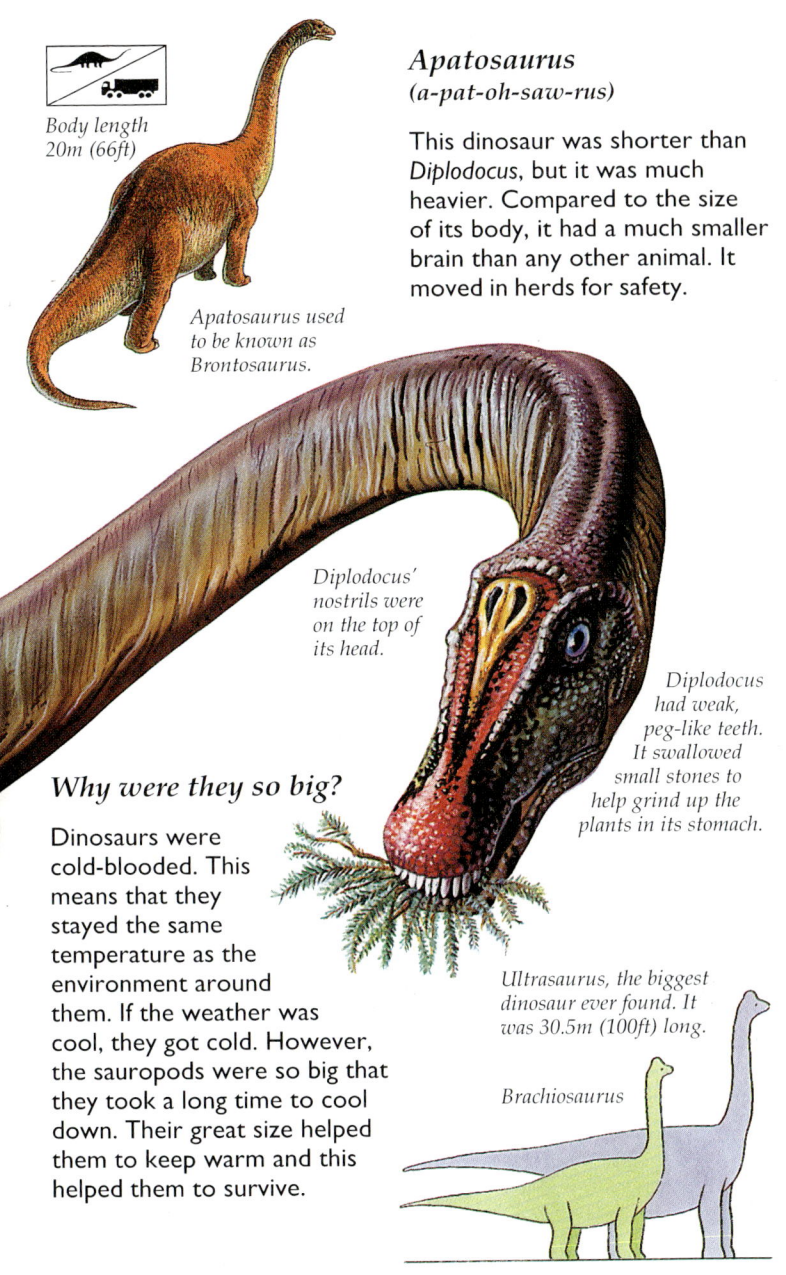

Body length
20m (66ft)

Apatosaurus used
to be known as
Brontosaurus.

Apatosaurus
(a-pat-oh-saw-rus)

This dinosaur was shorter than
Diplodocus, but it was much
heavier. Compared to the size
of its body, it had a much smaller
brain than any other animal. It
moved in herds for safety.

Diplodocus'
nostrils were
on the top of
its head.

Diplodocus
had weak,
peg-like teeth.
It swallowed
small stones to
help grind up the
plants in its stomach.

Why were they so big?

Dinosaurs were
cold-blooded. This
means that they
stayed the same
temperature as the
environment around
them. If the weather was
cool, they got cold. However,
the sauropods were so big that
they took a long time to cool
down. Their great size helped
them to keep warm and this
helped them to survive.

Ultrasaurus, the biggest
dinosaur ever found. It
was 30.5m (100ft) long.

Brachiosaurus

15

Crested dinosaurs

Hadrosaurs lived in the Cretaceous Period, which began 135 million years ago. Their top jaw was flattened at the tip and looked like a duck's bill. For this reason, they are also known as duck-billed dinosaurs.

Parasaurolophus
(parra-saw-rollo-fus)

This hadrosaur had an amazing crest on its head. The crest was made of curved, hollow bone, which contained complex air passages. It probably made noises by blowing air through its crest, hooting loudly to call a mate or scare enemies.

Other hadrosaurs

Hadrosaurs' bodies were very much alike, but each sort had a different shaped head. Here are some of them.

It stood on its back legs to run or to eat tall plants.

Body length 10m (33ft)

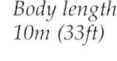

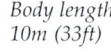

Tsintaosaurus (sinta-oh-saw-rus)

Kritosaurus (critto-saw-rus)

Saurolophus (saw-rollo-fuss)

This diagram shows how big *Parasaurolophus* was compared with a person.

Ceratopians

These dinosaurs also lived in the Cretaceous Period. They had parrot-like beaks, which they used to chop through the tough plants that they ate.

Body length 2m (7ft)

Psittacosaurus
(sitta-koh-saw-rus)

Most ceratopians walked on all fours, but this one was different. It walked on its back legs, but still had a parrot-like beak.

Leptoceratops
(lep-toe-ser-a-tops)

This was also unusual for a ceratopian. It was small and agile and ran on its back legs. It had a small frill on its neck and it had no horns, as it could run fast enough to escape from predators.

Body length 2m (7ft)

Body length 11m (36ft)

The name Triceratops means "three horned face".

Triceratops
(try-serra-tops)

Triceratops was the biggest ceratopian and also one of the last ones to exist. Its skull alone was 2m (7ft) long.

The big hunters

Big, meat-eating dinosaurs were called carnosaurs. They were enormous hunters with short arms, short necks and big heads. They walked on powerful back legs. They killed their prey with their feet or teeth.

Tyrannosaurus rex had a very strong, short neck.

Body height 5m (16ft)

Big wide feet had curved claws.

Tyrannosaurus rex
(tie-ranna-saw-rus rex)

This dinosaur's name means "tyrant lizard king". It was one of the biggest carnosaurs. It was 14m (46ft) long. It was so heavy that it could not run fast for very long. It probably waited for its prey and then made a quick attack.

Spinosaurus
(spy-no-saw-rus)

This carnosaur was unusual
in that it had a huge fin
stretching along its back. It
probably used its fin to
control its temperature. It
made itself warm by standing
with its fin facing the sun
and cooled itself down by
turning its fin away from
the sun.

*Spinosaurus probably ate
dead dinosaurs and may
have eaten fish too.*

Body length
8-16m
(26-52ft)

Ceratosaurus
(serra-toe-saw-rus)

This dinosaur had a small horn on
top of its head and bony ridges
over its eyes. Its name means
"horned reptile".

*Like other carnosaurs,
Ceratosaurus had small,
stumpy arms, which it
may have used for
holding prey.*

Horn

Body length
6m (20ft)

How big were they?

This diagram shows how
big *Tyrannosaurus rex*
and *Spinosaurus* were
compared with a
person.

19

Dome-headed dinosaurs

Dome-headed dinosaurs got their name from their dome-shaped skulls, which were made out of thick bone. These plant-eaters are also known as pachycephalosaurs.

Pachycephalosaurus
(packy-seffa-low-saw-rus)

This was the biggest dome-headed dinosaur. Its name means "thick-headed reptile". It had a very bumpy skull and bumps and spikes on its snout.

Body length 8m (26ft)

Thick skull cap protected its brain.

Bony bumps around dome.

Body length 3m (10ft)

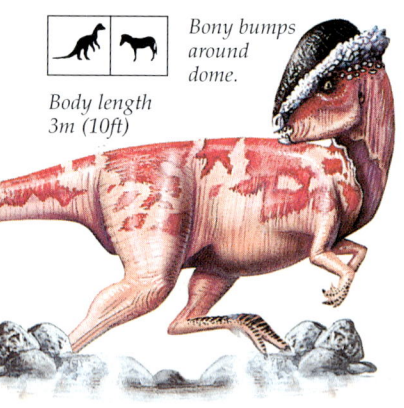

Stegoceras
(stegga-serras)

This was the first dome-headed dinosaur ever found. Not many *Stegoceras* remains have been found because they lived mainly in mountain areas, where few fossils were preserved.

Head-butting contests

Male dome-headed dinosaurs fought for leadership by head-butting each other.

They charged at each other again and again until the weaker dinosaur gave up.

Ornithopods

The ornithopod dinosaurs had bird-like feet and walked mainly on their back legs. They were all plant-eaters and had bird-like horny beaks for nipping off food.

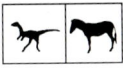

Body length 2m (7ft)

Hypsilophodon
(hips-ill-offa-don)

Hypsilophodon was a plant-eater. It was one of the smallest, but fastest dinosaurs. It was also very light.

Tail helped Hypsilophodon to balance.

Camptosaurus
(camp-toe-saw-rus)

Camptosaurus had hooves on its front and back legs. When it was being chased, it ran on its back legs. When it was grazing, it moved on all fours.

Body length 5m (16ft)

It had hooves on the ends of its fingers and toes.

Horny beak

Thumb claw

Iguanodon had powerful back legs and tail.

Iguanodon
(ig-wa-no-don)

This dinosaur had powerful back legs and tail. A sharp claw on each thumb was probably used as a weapon if an enemy came too close. The other fingers had hooves, so that it could walk on all fours.

Body length 10m (33ft)

21

Ankylosaurs

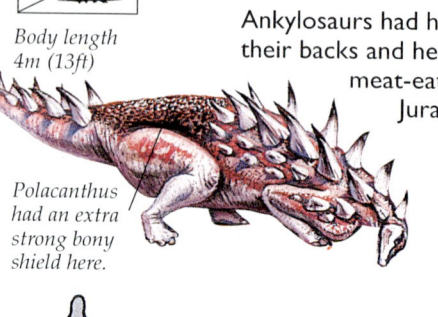

Body length
4m (13ft)

Ankylosaurs had heavy bony coverings on their backs and heads to protect them from meat-eaters. They lived in the late Jurassic and Cretaceous times, between 150 million and 65 million years ago.

Polacanthus had an extra strong bony shield here.

This picture shows how big *Polacanthus* was compared to a person.

Polacanthus
(polla-can-thus)

The underside of the ankylosaurs were unprotected. *Polacanthus* had long spikes along its sides and it probably crouched down when enemies approached.

Paleoscincus
(pay-lee-oh-skink-us)

This dinosaur had a very low body and short legs. Sharp spikes stuck out from the edges of its protective shield. This protected its legs and stomach.

Body length
6m (20ft)

Sharp
spikes

Thick, flexible,
bony plates.

Body length
4.5m (15ft)

Ankylosaurus
(anky-low-saw-rus)

This dinosaur's body was covered in a bony shield. Its name means "stiff reptile". It was slightly bigger than *Polacanthus*.

Stegosaurs

Stegosaurs were plant-eaters that lived in the Jurassic Period. They had large, bony plates sticking out of their backs and sharp tail spikes.

Stegosaurus
(stegga-saw-rus)

Stegosaurus was the biggest stegosaur. Scientists used to think that its plates were for defending itself, but it could be that they were for regulating its temperature, like Spinosaurus (see page 19).

Tail spikes could be used for stabbing enemies.

Body length 8m (26ft)

Stegosaurus' plates

Scientists used to think the plates on Stegosaurus' back lay flat like this.

Some then thought that the plates might be side-by-side in pairs along its back.

Now, many scientists think that the plates grew in two uneven rows along its back.

Kentrosaurus
(kent-roe-saw-rus)

Kentrosaurus was a smaller relative of Stegosaurus. If threatened, it would probably have turned its back on its enemy, which would have made an attack difficult.

It had a long spike on each side of its body.

Body length 5m (16ft)

Flying reptiles

At the same time that dinosaurs lived on land, one group of reptiles, called pterosaurs, used wings to fly. They were light, fragile reptiles.

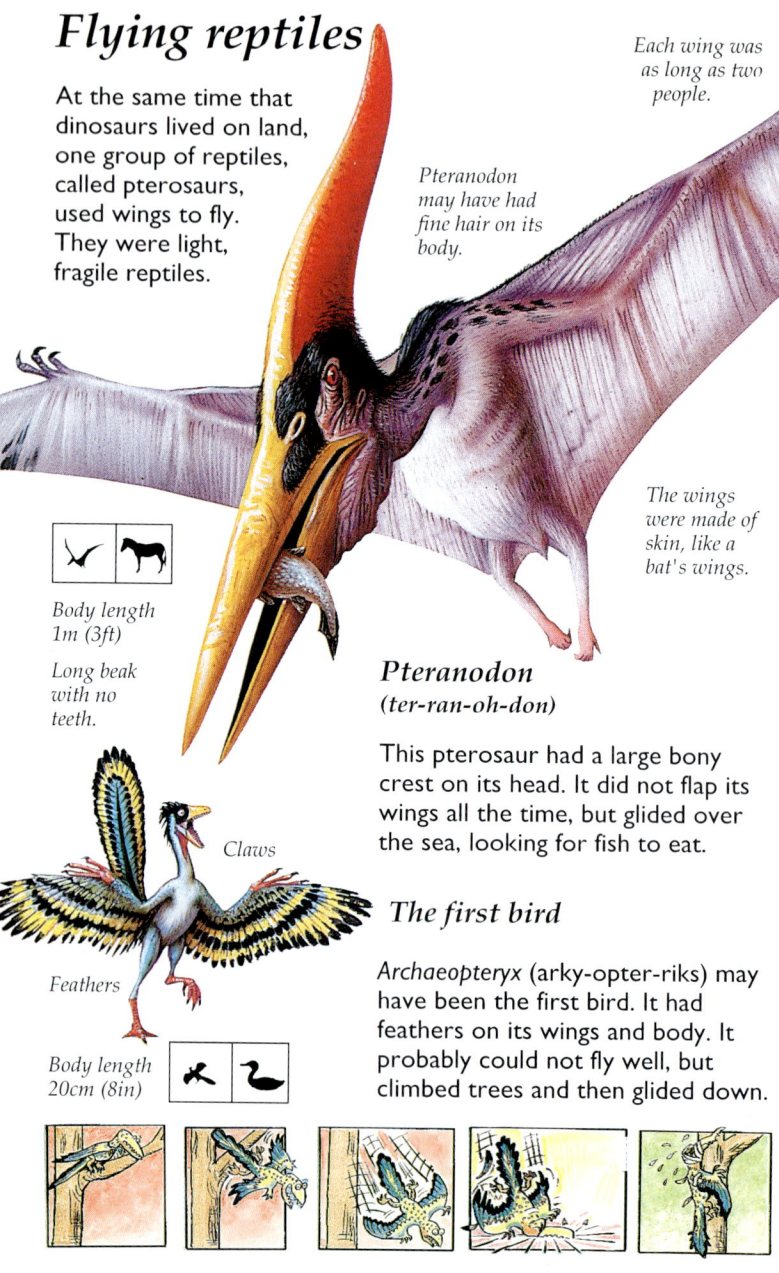

Each wing was as long as two people.

Pteranodon may have had fine hair on its body.

The wings were made of skin, like a bat's wings.

Body length 1m (3ft)

Long beak with no teeth.

Claws

Feathers

Body length 20cm (8in)

Pteranodon
(ter-ran-oh-don)

This pterosaur had a large bony crest on its head. It did not flap its wings all the time, but glided over the sea, looking for fish to eat.

The first bird

Archaeopteryx (arky-opter-riks) may have been the first bird. It had feathers on its wings and body. It probably could not fly well, but climbed trees and then glided down.

Sea reptiles

Groups of reptiles also lived in the sea during this time. Ichthyosaurs had similar shapes to the fish and dolphins of today, while other sea reptiles were less fish-like.

*Body length
2-9m (7-30ft)*

Plesiosaurus
(pleesy-oh-saw-rus)

This reptile swam slowly and flapped its flippers like a turtle. It fed on fish which it caught with quick movements of its long neck. Plesiosaurus pulled itself onto land to lay its eggs.

Flippers

Ichthyosaurus
(ik-thee-oh-saw-rus)

Icthyosaurus lived in the sea and was a fast swimmer. Its babies grew inside the mother and were born in the sea, like baby dolphins.

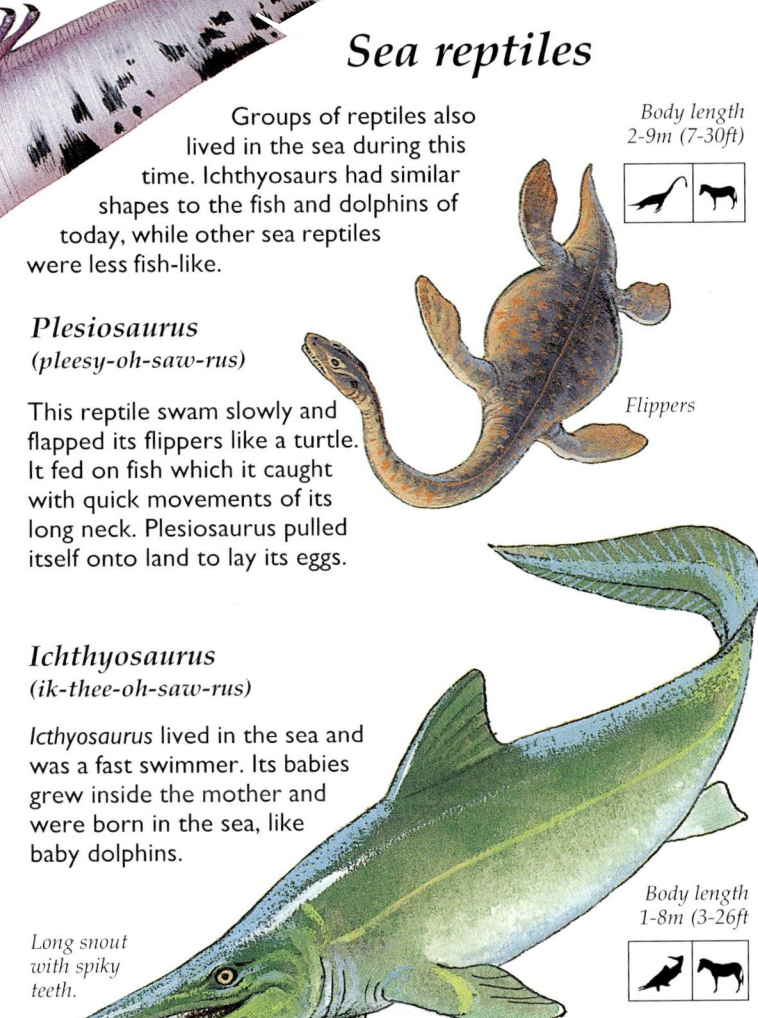

*Long snout
with spiky
teeth.*

*Body length
1-8m (3-26ft*

*Flippers used
for steering.*

This picture shows how big an *Ichthyosaurus* and a *Plesiosaurus* were compared with a person.

The end of the dinosaurs

The dinosaurs, sea reptiles and pterosaurs died out around 65 million years ago. No one knows for certain why this happened but there are a few theories.

One theory is that a star may have exploded close to our Solar System. This would have sent clouds of deadly radiation to Earth. Many animals would have died, or become damaged so that they could not reproduce.

Another theory is that as the continents began to separate around 195 million years ago, the oceans became larger. This produced a cooler climate. The cold-blooded dinosaurs would have been unable to keep warm and they might have died out.

Earth around 195 million years ago.

Earth around 64 million years ago.

The age of mammals begins

Although many kinds of animals died out at this time, some survived. Among them were the mammals. Mammals have fur or hair and give birth to live young. They are warm-blooded which means that they can control their body temperature.

Cynognathus was about 2m (7ft) long.

Cynognathus
(sine-og-naythus)

This was an early mammal. It looked a little like a dog and had several different types of teeth, as mammals do today.

The ice ages

Over the last few million years, there have been periods, called ice ages, when northern parts of the Earth were covered in ice. The most recent Ice Age began around two million years ago and ended around 10,000 years ago. Many animals, including people, adapted to living in these conditions.

Smilodon used its long, stabbing teeth to tear the thick skin of its prey.

Smilodon (smill-oh-don), also known as a sabre-toothed cat, lived at the start of the last Ice Age. It was fierce and may have hunted woolly mammoths.

Woolly mammoths were about 4½m (15ft) tall.

Long tusks enabled them to scrape away snow and uncover plants to eat.

Woolly mammoths

Woolly mammoths lived in the last Ice Age. They were similar to the elephants of today. They had long woolly hair and a layer of fat under their skin to keep them warm.

Prehistoric time chart

The history of life on Earth is split up into eras, and the eras are divided into periods. The age of the dinosaurs spanned three periods – the Triassic, Jurassic and Cretaceous. The dinosaurs did not all live at the same time. Some died out before others had yet evolved.

Era	Period	Years ago (millions)	
Mesozoic	Cretaceous	64 135	Birds, Ornithomimus, Tyrannosaurus, Deinonychus, Ceratosaurus
	Jurassic	195	Archaeopteryx, Compsognathus, Mammals, Coelophysis
	Triassic	225	Megazostrodon, Coelophysis
Palaeozoic	Permian	280	Amphibians, Seymouria, Diplocaulus
	Carboniferous	345	
	Devonian	395	Eusthenopteron
	Silurian	440	Cephalaspis (jawless fish)
	Ordovician	500	Cup coral
	Cambrian	600	Hallucigenia

Age of reptiles

Age of fish

This tree-like time chart shows how dinosaurs are related to one another, and to some other prehistoric animals. The animals on each small branch of the tree evolved from the animals on the larger branch from which it divided. All dinosaurs evolved from a group of primitive archosaur reptiles (see page 7).

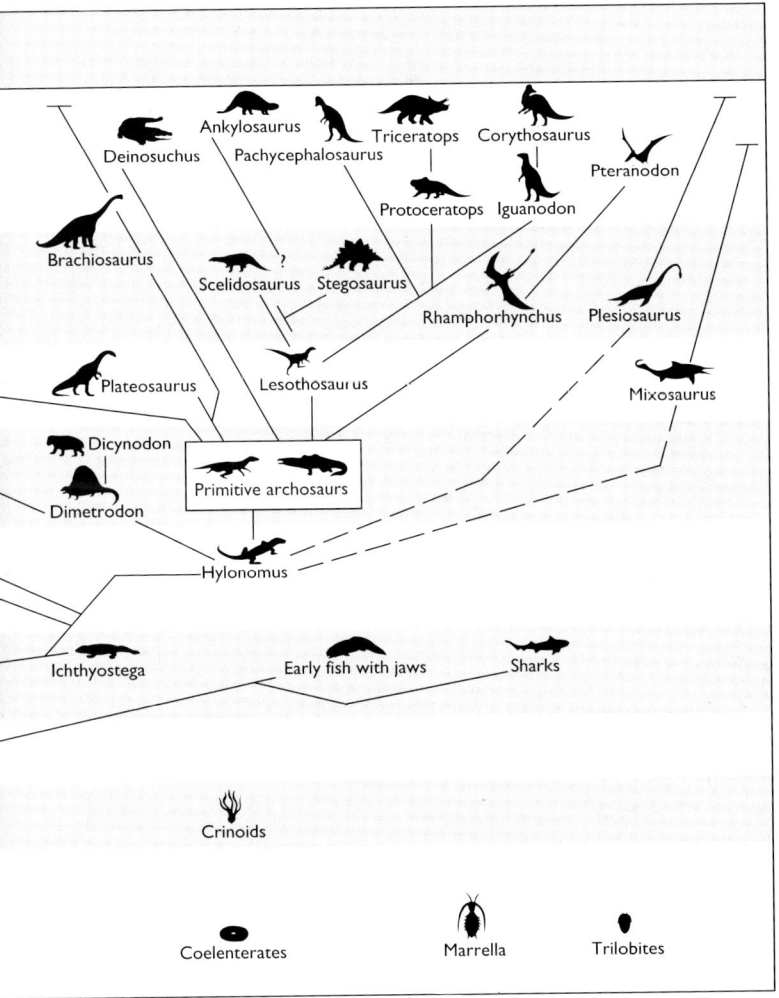

Deinosuchus

Ankylosaurus
Pachycephalosaurus

Triceratops   Corythosaurus

Pteranodon

Protoceratops   Iguanodon

Brachiosaurus

Scelidosaurus   Stegosaurus

Rhamphorhynchus   Plesiosaurus

Plateosaurus   Lesothosaurus

Mixosaurus

Dicynodon

Primitive archosaurs

Dimetrodon

Hylonomus

Ichthyostega   Early fish with jaws   Sharks

Crinoids

Coelenterates   Marrella   Trilobites

Prehistoric checklist

Here is a quick guide to the animals featured in this book.

Name (pronunciation)	Meaning of name	Where found	When it lived		
			Tri-assic	Jurassic	Cretaceous
Ankylosaurus (anky-low-saw-rus)	Stiff reptile	North America			
Apatosaurus (a-pat-oh-saw-rus)	Headless reptile	North America			
Archaeopteryx (arky-opter-riks)	Ancient wing	Europe			
Brachiosaurus (bracky-oh-saw-rus)	Arm reptile	North America			
Camptosaurus (camp-toe-saw-rus)	Flexible reptile	Great Britain & North America			
Ceratosaurus (serra-toe-saw-rus)	Horned reptile	North America			
Coelophysis (see-low-fie-sis)	Hollow face	Mexico			
Compsognathus (comp-sog-nay-thus)	Pretty jaw	Germany			
Deinonychus (die-nonny-kus)	Terrible claw	USA			
Dimetrodon (dee-mee-tro-don)	Two-sized tooth	USA	Pre-Triassic		
Diplodocus (dip-low-doe-kus)	Double beam	North America			
Euoplocephalus (you-oh-plo-seffa-lus)	True-plated head	North America			
Eusthenopteron (use-then-opter-ron)	True narrow fin	Greenland	Pre-Triassic		
Heterodontosaurus (hetter-roe-donta-saw-rus)	Mixed-tooth reptile	South Africa			
Hypsilophodon (hips-ill-offa-don)	High-ridged tooth	North America			
Ichthyosaurus (ik-thee-oh-saw-rus)	Fish reptile	Europe			
Iguanodon (ig-wa-no-don)	Iguana tooth	Europe & North America			
Kentrosaurus (kent-roe-saw-rus)	Prickly reptile	Tanzania			

Index

This book is based on material previously published in *The Usborne Book of Dinosaurs* and the *Usborne Spotter's Guide to Dinosaurs* and the *Usborne Children's Encyclopedia of Prehistoric Life*.

First published in 1995 by Usborne Publishing Ltd, Usborne House, 83-85 Saffron Hill, London EC1N 8RT, England.

UE   First published in America August 1995.

Printed in Italy.

Name (pronunciation)	Meaning of name	Where found	When it lived		
			Tri-assic	Jurassic	Cretaceous
Kritosaurus (critto-saw-rus)	Reptile from Kirtland	Kirtland, USA			
Leptoceratops (lep-toe-ser-a-tops)	Slender-horned face	North America			
Lesothosaurus (less-oh-toe-saw-rus)	Reptile from Lesotho	Lesotho, Africa			
Ornithosuchus (or-nith-oh-sook-us)	Bird-like crocodile	Great Britain	Pre-Triassic		
Pachycephalosaurus (packy-seffa-low-saw-rus)	Thick-headed reptile	Canada			
Parasaurolophus (parra-saw-rollo-fus)	Reptile with parallel-sided crest	North America			
Plateosaurus (platty-oh-saw-rus)	Flat reptile	Southern Germany			
Plesiosaurus (pleesy-oh-saw-rus)	Ribbon reptile	Europe			
Polacanthus (polla-can-thus)	Many spined	Great Britain			
Psittacosaurus (sitta-koh-saw-rus)	Parrot reptile	Mongolia			
Pteranodon (ter-ran-oh-don)	Winged and toothless	North America			
Rhamphorhynchus (ram-foe-rin-kus)	Beak nose	Southern Germany			
Saurolophus (saw-rollo-fuss)	Ridged reptile	Mongolia & North America			
Spinosaurus (spy-no-saw-rus)	Spiny reptile	Egypt			
Stegosaurus (stegga-saw-rus)	Roofed reptile	North America			
Stegoceras (stegga-serras)	Horned roof (skull)	North America			
Triceratops (try-serra-tops)	Three-horned face	North America			
Tsintaosaurus (sinta-oh-saw-rus)	Reptile from Tsintao	Tsintao, China			
Tyrannosaurus rex (tie-ranna-saw-rus rex)	Tyrant reptile king	USA			

31